Pico and the Golden Lagoon

By Sally Miller and Jesse Hamilton
Artwork by John Davis

Story adapted from the the original puppet show
Pico and the Golden Lagoon
By Pico's Puppet Palace

ISBN: 978-0-646-83973-8

A catalogue record for this work is available from the National Library of Australia

Pico and the Golden Lagoon

Somewhere off the coast,
way out there beyond the horizon,
where the sea pours into the ocean
and the great winds collide,
where hardly anyone ever goes,
and hardly anyone even knows,
there lies an island hidden in time,
charmed by the sun and draped in gold.
You won't find it on any map,
and you can't go there directly.
Rather, you have to end up
carried there on the currents,
                    one way or another.

"MAYDAY, MAYDAY

This is Pico to home base,
Pico to homebase!
I'm lost. My compass is going crazy,
and I'm running out of fuel.
Pico to home base, do you copy?
I'm running out of fuel.
I think I'm going to have to make a crash landing.
Pico to home base, can you hear me?
I can't hold on any longer.
Pico to home base,

HHHEEELLLPPP!!!"

Pico lay sprawled out on the beach, just a few short steps from her plane. The dust was still settling all around her when she came to. She opened her eyes and couldn't believe it. "I'm alive," she gasped. "I'm ALIVE!..." But where was she? What was this strange place? "Is there anybody out there? Can anyone hear me? Help," she cried, "HELP!"

But no one replied.

She sat up, took a deep breath, and looked around. Before her, rising up like a wall, stood a dense, impenetrable jungle. Behind her, stretching out endlessly, the blue sea lapped calmly on the shore. There was no sign of civilization, no sign of people. Pico got a sinking feeling she was all alone, and very far from home. Her good fortune was quickly turning to despair, and she was on the verge of tears, when suddenly, from out of the jungle, like a shining beacon, a spectacular, huge, golden yellow dragonfly appeared! It flew right over to where she was sitting and hovered inquisitively before her face, humming loudly.

"Oh hello," said Pico, surprised. "Would you look at that - a dragonfly, and it's enormous! I've never seen one like that before. Well, it looks like there is life on the island after all. I'm in luck!"

The dragonfly hung in the air before her a moment longer, as though it was trying to tell her something. Then abruptly, it snapped its shimmering wings, and zipped off back into the jungle.

"Hey, where are you going?" Pico called out. "Where are you going?" Then, on a moment's impulse, she picked herself up from the sands and decided to chase after it. In hot pursuit she ran into the woods yelling, "hey wait for me, WAIT FOR ME!"

Meanwhile, on another part of the island, not too far away, other signs of life were beginning to emerge from the bush.

"Good morning Renard," greeted the wolf.

"Oh good morning Lupe," replied the fox. "How are you today?"

"Oh my allergies, my allergies," complained the wolf with a tremendous sneeze. "My allergies!"

"Well, I've told you time and time again Lupe, if you keep sniffing those flowers, you'll keep getting those allergies."

But the wolf wouldn't be changed. "I like sniffing flowers Renard," he said. "They smell so good!"

The fox smiled patiently. He knew his friend too well. "I know you do Lupe," he said. "I know you do."

"Oh hey, Renard?" asked the wolf.

"Yes, Lupe," answered the fox, raising his eyebrows.

"What's the time?"

The fox rolled his eyes. "Oh you silly wolf," he said. "Everyone knows it's island time."

The wolf didn't understand. "Island time, what's that?" he asked.

"Well," the fox explained. "It means it's a good time to sit back, relax, and take in the scenery."

The wolf still didn't get it. "That's a bit boring isn't it?"

"No," replied the fox. "I find it quite relaxing, actually."

The wolf wasn't convinced, but he left it at that. "Oh hey, Renard?" he asked again.

"Yes, Lupe," sighed the fox, losing patience.

"Do you know what I saw this morning, while I was on the beach, looking for food along the high water line? I saw the strangest thing. I saw a big yellow bird with four wings."

"Four wings?" scoffed the fox. "Couldn't have been. Everyone knows birds don't have four wings. They've only got two. Perhaps it was a dragonfly? Dragonflies have got four wings."

"No," insisted the wolf. "This was a bird. It was big, yellow, and it had four wings."

"Must have been a dragonfly," repeated the fox.

"Oh come on Renard, come down to the beach and I'll show you."

"No," said the fox. "I was planning on doing absolutely nothing today."

"Oh, come on Renard," pleaded the wolf. "Please?"

The fox knew his friend would never give up. "Fine," he said. "Come and show me this big yellow bird with four wings."

"Oh, come on then," led the wolf, and the two scampered off towards the beach.

Back on the path, Pico was getting more and more turned around. The jungle was an endless maze of trails leading nowhere. Every crossroads looked the same as the last. No one was answering her calls. She couldn't even see any animals, and there was no sign of that dragonfly. She was tired, hungry, and lost, and was beginning to think the island was deserted. She could barely see the point, but she pushed on, telling herself, "must, keep, going."

And while Pico was busy chasing her tail in the forest, high above it all, up on the crest, another resident of the island was just finishing breakfast, and getting on with the day's work. Yes, there was nothing David quite liked better than sitting in his jungle headquarters, and looking for birds. And today, he was looking for the rare, Giant Sunil Parrot - often spotted this time of the year in the tops of the trees. With his trusty binoculars, he scanned the forest for hints of blue and yellow - the parrot's tell tale colours. Back and forth he peered - but no. It looked like he was fresh out of luck. "Ah well," he told himself. "Plenty of other birds to spot," and carried on his search. This time, he took his binoculars on a long, slow pass over towards the beach, when suddenly, something brilliant yellow filled his view. His eyes bulged right out of his head. "By golly!" he exclaimed. "What is that down by the lagoon?" He took another long look, and it could only have been one of two things. Either it was a rather large dragonfly, or, it was a little yellow biplane. David focused his binoculars once more to be sure, and sure enough, it had to be the second option - a little yellow biplane. Why, he'd never seen a little yellow biplane, in this neck of the woods, well, ever, actually. Oh, he had been planning on spotting birds all day, but he figured he'd best go down and see if there was a pilot in distress. So off to the lagoon he went.

Marooned, all on her own, and at her wits'
end, Pico was lost. There was no denying it.
She was just going around in circles. She was
overwhelmed, afraid, and exhausted. Indeed,
she was in distress. She just wanted to close
her eyes and wake up at home. She cried, but
no one could hear her. No one could help.
She just couldn't take another step. So she
decided to have a little nap, right there against a
nearby tree. She plonked herself down, and no
sooner had she laid her head against its trunk,
her troubles all fell away, and she was snoring
loudly.

David, however, hadn't managed to get very far, before he got held up by the croak of some frog - a Grassalum Frog he presumed, but he'd have to see it to be sure. Yes, that was the marvellous thing about this island - you couldn't go very far before you discovered some new kind of plant or animal. But where was it? David searched. The croaking seemed to be coming from everywhere. He looked high and low, left and right, but where, where? He stood still and listened, and then, there, there it was, right under his nose. David bent over to have a close up look at its markings. It blended right into the forest floor with its perfect camouflage. Only its croaking gave it away. And it was just as he suspected - the small Grassalum Frog. "Oh well," he told himself. "Enough distractions, on to the little yellow biplane I go."

But no sooner had he said it, was he distracted all over again - this time, by a rather superb looking butterfly fluttering across the path. He froze in his tracks. "I do believe," he whispered, "that is the long distance migrating, Blue Mariposa." The graceful butterfly danced elegantly before him, and David was spellbound, as slowly, it began to waft his way, flitting closer and closer, till finally, it landed right on the end of his nose. He stood absolutely still. This had never happened to him before. The butterfly rested there for a moment while David held his breath, and then, all at once, it flapped its delicate wings and resumed its dance, fluttering away into the forest. David shook his head in wonder - never a dull moment! "Anyways," he said. "Off to the lagoon I go."

Pico was sound asleep, soaring the heavens in her biplane and doing loop de loops above the clouds, when upon her along the path came David. He spotted the young pilot napping there against a tree, snoring away. He decided to go up and gently wake her, so as not to scare her too much. Creeping near, he cleared his throat.

"Ahem."

Pico woke with a jolt. She didn't know where she was. She looked around desperately, in real fear, and then she saw David standing over her, and she knew she was saved. "I'm saved!" she yelled. "I'M SAVED! I found a real person. I FOUND A REAL PERSON!"

"Well, of course I'm a real person," spoke David, matter-of-factly. "I'm David."

Pico was overjoyed - what luck, and just when she'd lost all hope. "Hi David," she blurted out. "I'm Pico, and boy am I glad to see you." Then in a blither, she proceeded to tell him all about her crash landing and how she got lost in the jungle, winding up, faster and faster as she went. Well, she must have been speaking a million miles an hour, because suddenly David cut her off, abruptly.

"Calm down," he said. "Take a deep breath."

Pico did as she was told, and took a huge, deep breath, exhaling out, down to the very bottom of her lungs.

"Now," continued David, "start from the beginning, but please, a little slower this time."

Pico started again, much calmer. "Hi David," she said. "I'm Pico, and you see, I was in my plane on my mail run, when my compass went crazy. I went way off course, ran out of fuel, and had to make a crash landing. I've been walking around in the jungle for hours. I got tired, had a nap, but now I've found you, and I'm saved. I'M SAVED! Because, well, I need some fuel for my plane, and you, you David, you can lend me some, right?"

A shadow fell over David's face. "I'm sorry Pico," he apologised. "I can't lend you any fuel."

"Oh, why's that?" Pico asked, surprised.

"Because Pico," he said finally, "I don't have any."

Pico's heart sank, but there was still a chance. "Well," she asked, "maybe there's someone else on this island who can lend me some fuel?"

"No, Pico," David replied. "There's no one else on this island - just me."

Pico's jaw dropped. "Just you?" she said. "But how did you even get here David?"

"Well Pico," the old man began. "It was a long time ago…."

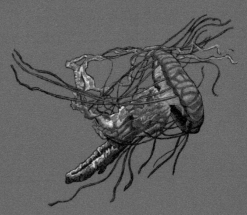

"**I** was a young Naturalist, on an expedition in my canoe, looking for an ancient species of electric, iridescent jellyfish. We were out on the Caribbean Sea, when all of a sudden, the sky turned black, and a big wind came up and swept me away from the rest of my group. I was cast away at sea for days. I was starving, dehydrated, and I'd almost lost hope. When, in the distance, I saw the faint outline of some trees. I used the last of my energy and paddled towards those trees, and came ashore on this island not far from here, and like you Pico, I thought, 'by golly I'm saved!' But nobody came to save me. I lit fires for smoke signals. I looked into the sky for rescue planes. I watched the horizon for ships, but nobody came. Days turned into weeks. Weeks turned into months. Months turned into years. My hair turned grey! But you know Pico, after all that time, I started to really love this island. You see - there's so many new species of animals, plants, and birds. I would need ten lifetimes to document them all, and there's no loud noises, no stinky fumes - *no fuel*, just me, and paradise."

Pico listened in amazement to David's thrilling tale of survival - to have lived all those years alone on the island! She could hardly imagine it. It was only after he finished speaking did it even occur to her. "Um, David?" she asked quietly. "If there's no fuel, then how am I going to fly my plane? How am I going to LEAVE?"

David spelled it out to her. "Well Pico," he said, "you might just have to stay."

"STAY! I can't stay here. I've got places to be - people to see! I've still got PARCELS TO DELIVER!"

David shook his head. "I'm sorry Pico. I can't help you."

Pico was desperate. "Think David, THINK!" she implored him. "There must be some way."

For a long while, David scratched his head in silence, thinking. Then slowly, a little light went on in his mind. "Well, there could be one option," he ventured cautiously, "perhaps?"

"Yes," said Pico, clutching his arm.

David pulled his arm away. "No actually," he said. "forget I mentioned it. It's too risky."

But Pico wouldn't have it. "What? David you can't tell me there might be one option, and then tell me to forget you mentioned it. You have to tell me."

"No," he said firmly. "It's too risky - just drop it Pico."

Pico pleaded with her eyes, tears welling. "Please David," she begged.

David gazed down at the pitiful young pilot, and then finally, softening, he sighed. "Oh all right then Pico, listen. On this island there is a lagoon."

"A lagoon?" she asked.

"Yes, and at the edge of this lagoon there is a cave."

"A cave?" she followed him, eyes widening.

"Yes, and inside this cave, there lives a dragon."

"A DRAGON!" she exclaimed.

"Yes, a dragon," continued David, "and this dragon, she guards a treasure - **gold treasure**."

"GOLD TREASURE!" echoed Pico.

"Yes," said David, "But it's no ordinary gold. This gold is special. This gold is **photovoltaic**!"

"PHOTOCASLAIC!" sniggered Pico. "I've never heard of that before."

"No Pico," David corrected her. "I said PHOTOVOLTAIC. Photo means light, and Volt means electricity. So that means, this gold absorbs the sun's light and converts it into electricity. You see, I figure - you get some of this gold, sprinkle it on your plane, and your plane will become powered by the sun. Why, it will become a SOLAR POWERED BIPLANE!"

Pico keeled over with laughter. It was the funniest thing she'd ever heard - as if her plane could be powered by the energy of the sun.

"It's not funny Pico!" snapped David. "Take a look around you. Everything on this island is powered by the sun."

Pico smartened up. "It is?" she asked.

"Sure," he said, only too happy to explain. "Just take a look around you…"

"The sun shines down on the island, and the plants catch this light with their leaves, and they can use this light to make energy. It's called *photosynthesis*!"

"Photosynthesis?" stumbled Pico.

"Yes that right," David nodded, "and the plants use this photo energy to grow, and they grow big, and produce fruit. Then I come along and eat the fruit, and the animals eat the fruit. It helps spread the seeds, and so more plants grow. And among them, the animals find their homes, and I too can cut them down to build things like my jungle headquarters, and it's all because of the energy of the sun."

Just then, standing there in the middle of that thick jungle, with the sun pouring down, and the plants all around her stretching their leaves out like hands trying to catch it, Pico could see the evidence of David's words plain as day, and she was just about on board for the adventure. She still had one little, nagging question though. "Um, David," she asked, "it sounds like a plan, but how am I going to get the treasure, if it's guarded by a *dragon*?"

"Ah yes, the dragon," said David.

"Ah yeah David, the DRAGON," said Pico.

But the old man had a plan. "Well ordinarily Pico," he said, "this dragon, she fiercely guards her treasure, but once every full moon, she comes out of her cave, and is so intoxicated by the moon's generous light, she does a wild full moon dance with her reflection in the lagoon, and at that moment, with anyone who is bold enough to ask, she'll gladly share her treasure."

Pico perked up. "Oh that's great," she said. "When's the next full moon David?"

"Why it's in three days time Pico."

"Three days!" groaned Pico. "You mean I have to stay on this island for three whole days?"

"Well it's the only way she'll give you the treasure," David assured her. "And I tell you, after those three days, you won't want to leave. I'm going to show you what island life is really like. Come on, the fun starts here."

"Oh all right then," grumbled Pico, dragging her heels.

Well, David didn't exaggerate. Every glorious morning on the island was a marvel to wake up to. Pico and David spent the first part of their days watching birds from David's jungle headquarters. They swapped the binoculars between them, while David took notes. There were so many different birds, and David knew them all! Pico was amazed. She had never really paid much attention to birds, even though she herself was a flier. But there was one bird David hadn't been able to spot, and that was the Giant Sunil Parrot, and this was the season for it. Pico had a good feeling about it though. "Don't worry David," she said. "We'll

spot that parrot."

Afternoons they spent traipsing along the many paths, combing the beaches, and watching out for critters along the way! They climbed trees, and peered into nests to see how the chicks were coming along. From up top, they gazed out over the forest canopy, and there was lots of room to roam!

When it came time for lunch, David would smirk, and say, "Come on now, off to the shops," and he would lead Pico out to gather nuts and fruits from the different trees and bushes. Somehow David knew which ones you could eat, and when to pick them. How did he know? "Well, I've been watching birds for a long time now," he said, "and I've learned quite a few tricks from them." David was a real birder, through and through.

Yes, days passed like these. Time was a ritual that changed with the seasons. "When fruits are ripe, it's best to pick them," said David. Luckily, with so many distractions, it never felt like work. The island held something new around every turn.

And it was like this one afternoon - which afternoon? Was it the third already? (Pico had stopped counting.) The two had gone to pick pine nuts at the very heart of the island, and they had come to the base of a towering old conifer. As they approached its enormous trunk, pinecones began falling from the branches above, landing with heavy thumps on the forest floor.

David got excited and pointed up. "Look Pico," he called. "I think I've spotted that parrot!"

Pico looked up, and right there above them, in full view, was the elusive, Giant Sunil Parrot, in full regalia! If you counted its tail feathers, the bird was nearly long as Pico was tall. Its chest was yellow as Pico's biplane, and its wings were a deep blue oceans and skies with hints of green and gold. As Pico "oohed" and "ahhed," the parrot stopped, tilted its head to the side, and peered one glassy black eye down at her, and winked!

"Look, she's smiling!" laughed Pico.

"Yes," said David. "These birds are extremely good natured." And to further prove the point, he hurriedly began gathering up the unfinished cones the bird was dropping. "I'd swear she's sharing with us," he said, pointing out her habit of sampling one, before dropping it and moving on to the next. "She's a great distributor of seeds!" he added.

Eventually, the parrot tired of eating, and perching on a low branch, she began preening herself with her massive black beak. She displayed all her finery for Pico and David, spreading her tail out like a great fan. Until finally, she stretched her powerful wings, sounded a deafening screech, and took to the sky, beating the air as she went. They could feel the wind below as she took off.

Pico was in awe, and David was too. It was a very good omen, and as they set about gathering up all the cones, they could feel the island's blessing. It didn't take long before they had a tremendous pile, and by the time they had finished picking all the seeds from them, both their pouches were full. Their work was finished. It was time to go.

"Come on Pico," David called. "Let's go take a nap."

"But I'm not tired," cried Pico.

"Yes, but you know what tonight is?" he reminded her. "It's the full moon. And tonight we go in my canoe across the lagoon to get the treasure. So come on, it's a big journey. We'd better rest up."

Pico sighed reluctantly, "Oh, all right then, I'm coming."

It was now late in the day, and the sun was dipping low into the ocean. The sky was bronze and gold and flaming orange, and Renard and Lupe were just stepping out of the bushes to have one last run of the beaches before the sun went down. They had just overheard the old man and the young flyer speaking in the forest, and Lupe couldn't believe it. Were they actually going to meet the dragon?

"Yes, they are going to get the treasure," confirmed Renard.

Lupe stuck his tail between his legs. "But I'd be scared to ask a dragon for treasure - dragons are scary!"

"Yes, but you remember," the fox reassured him, "every full moon she comes out of her cave, and does that dance, and she isn't scary at all."

The wolf's face lit up. "Oh I do remember," he said. "Hey, can we go watch from the bushes like last time?"

Renard eyed the wolf. "Well," he asked, "have you been sniffing flowers? Because you know, if you do, it aggravates your allergies, and if you sneeze, you'll give away our hiding spot in the bushes!"

Lupe confessed. "I maybe just sniffed one or two, but that was a long time ago. I promise I'll hold my sneezes in. Please Renard?"

Renard just couldn't resist the wolf. "Oh all right," he said, "come on, it's getting dark."

Night fell, and Pico must have been tired after all. When David came to wake her, it took her a few moments to realize where she was - lying there on a mattress of reeds, beneath a ceiling of thatched palm and bamboo in David's jungle headquarters. "Come on Pico," he called gently. "The moon is about to rise."

Pico rubbed the sleep from her eyes and followed him outside. Together they walked along the shadowy path through the forest to the clearing where David kept his canoe by the lagoon. They took their paddles, placed the boat upon the water, and climbed in. Before them, the moon rose - great on the horizon from her chambers beneath the sea. Her light spread out across the water, and she seemed so close. Pico could see every detail of her face, and she almost thought she could hear her voice.

"*I am the Moon*," she seemed to murmur, "and I have all the time in the world. From across the skies I summon the tides, and by ebb and flow, I am here to guide you. People like to think I'm there, even when they're not looking at me. They come out of their houses to tell stories in the square, children chase their shadows, and even magical dragons come out of their cave to dance in their own special way. *I am the Moon.*"

Pico and David set out across the lagoon, and as they dipped their paddles, their strokes left swirling eddies of green light in the water behind them; for the lagoon was awash with a glowing phosphorescent algae that thrived in its warm waters, and every splash set off sparks. Fish fleeing before the canoe's path left bright streaks, and over onshore, everywhere in the shadows, glow bugs too were dancing along with the croaking frogs, and the cicadas with their castanets. It was like a festival of lights.

"It's what I like to call the Disco of the Night," said David. "It's nature's way of throwing us a party."

Pico shook her head in wonder. She had never seen anything like it. And then, as they paddled further, thousands of little silver fish began leaping out of the water around them, scales flashing in the moonlight like a magic mirror ball. Some even landed in the canoe. "Um, David," Pico asked. "What are these fish leaping into the boat?"

"Well I do believe they are a distant relative of the Piranha," he replied.

"A PIRANHA!" shrieked Pico.

"Yes, they do this every full moon," he said calmly. "They throw themselves out of the water to try and reach her glow. But don't worry. They won't hurt you. Just gently pick them up and put them back in the water."

Pico took a close look at their fearsome teeth, and then quickly dropped the fish back in the water. Then she and David pressed on across the lagoon, till finally, the far shore neared.

David ceased paddling and raised his voice once more. "Ok Pico, looks like we're almost there," he said. "So what's going to happen is, I'm going to pull the canoe up to the shore, and you're going to go up to the cave and ask the dragon for the treasure."

Pico was confused. "You mean you're not going to come with me?" she asked.

"No," said David, "she'll only give you the treasure if you go alone."

Pico clung to the canoe. "But I'm scared to go alone," she cried.

"Well it's the only way. You'll just have to muscle up the courage," he said pointing to shore. "Look out Pico, we've arrived!"

The canoe drifted up on the sands, and Pico hopped out to catch the bow. Standing with her feet in the water she pushed David back out to the deep, then bravely turned, and scrambled her way up the beach. She was tingling with fear all over, and her feet would barely obey her, but she forced her way, creeping along the dunes until she came upon the cave's open mouth. She crouched down, and watched with dread the gaping entrance. The moon had risen to the top of sky, and her silver reflection was now long, stretching out across the water. Pico peered deep into the cave's darkness, and there she thought she glimpsed, sparks of yellow and gold, and something, someone, moving within. Pico held her breath as gradually, a great lumbering form emerged, swinging her head from side to side, and looking up to the moon. The dragon - Lou, showed herself.

Well, Lou wasn't exactly what Pico had been expecting; was she even a dragon, or maybe some prehistoric, upright crocodile - the last of her kind? Her long tail swished behind her in the sand, and her rows of gleaming white teeth shone in the moonlight - but they weren't the sharp, piercing teeth of a meat eater. They were the flat, grinding kind of a plant eater - for Lou was a herbivore, much to Pico's relief. Still, the lizard was formidable, so Pico kept hidden. Laying low behind a tuft of reeds, she watched as the dragon lumbered down to the water's edge, and that's when something truly weird occured! Glimpsing her own reflection cast on the lagoon by the full moon light, Lou began to sway - just her head at first, then gradually

her shoulders, her hips, and all the way down to her knees. Then she began to shuffle and stamp her feet, until getting more and more carried away, she reeled round and round in circles in a joyful frenzy, dancing in partners with her mirrored self. She shook her tail like you shake yours. She threw her head back and wagged out her tongue. Stepping side to side, she did a little shimmy, got real low, and then reached her arms to the sky! All to some inner music we can only imagine, and Pico witnessed it all. For this was the dragon's night out, just to dance, and forget about everything, and Lou was giving herself a proper shaking down. It was quite a sight, and it went on long into the night, but little by little, lower and lower, the moon fell from the sky, and the dragon's reflection began to retreat, further and further from the shore. And so, saving her slow dance for last, Lou brought the tempo down. Who knew dragons had such grace? Pico watched in disbelief as Lou swayed in the moonlight. Until finally, the music faded, and the dragon just stood there, waving her little forearms farewell - her partner, now just a shimmer in the far distance.

Pico saw this was her chance, and she had to act fast. Stepping up from behind the reeds, she went to greet the dragon, but Lou, still in a trance, didn't see her. She had to speak up in a loud voice. "Hi, I'm Pico," she announced.

The dragon's eyes snapped around quick, and for a terrifying moment, she beheld the young pilot. This was something she hadn't expected. Then in a deep, not at all unfriendly voice, she introduced herself. "Well hello Pico," she said. "I'm Lou, and how are you?"

Pico stammered. "I'm, I'm, I'm f,f,f,fine thank you. How are you?"

"Oh I'm great," reported Lou, "thanks for asking." Then, bringing her snout down to Pico's level, the great lizard met with her eyes. "And how is it that you got here?" she asked.

Pico shielded her face from the dragon's breath with her hands, then spat it out, "I came across the lagoon in the canoe with David!"

The dragon, hearing the old man's name, chuckled. "Oh David," she spoke fondly. "How is David?"

"Um, he's good," replied Pico, cautiously, but gaining confidence. "He said that you, well, that you…," where she hesitated once more, "that you, you have, some, *treasure*?" she asked, finally.

The dragon broke out laughing. "Treasure? Oh Sure, I've got some treasure. Would you like some of my treasure?" she asked.

Pico couldn't believe it. "What, you mean you're just going to give me your treasure like that?"

"Sure kid," bellowed Lou. "What's mine is yours!"

It seemed crazy to Pico, but the full moon always made Lou feel like that - like dancing around in circles and giving away everything. Pico had timed it perfectly. "Well actually, yes, I would like some of your treasure," she admitted.

"Well," Lou offered, "come back into my cave. I'll give you the treasure, and then I'll give you a ride across the lagoon on my back."

Pico was still a little afraid, and she didn't want to push her luck. "No, that's alright," she said politely. "I'll just go back across in the canoe with David."

"Oh come on Pico," insisted Lou. "How often is it that you get to ride on the back of a dragon?"

Pico had to think. "….Um, never," she said. "I've never had that opportunity before."

"Well come on then. We'll get the treasure, and I'll give you a ride!"

And in a moment of daring, Pico agreed. "Ok, sure," she said.

Pico followed the ambling lizard back into her darkened den, and stepped right into a chamber of golden light - not bright, but low, and softly pulsing. Pico looked at what was before her. It was a mountain of gold, the place dripping in gold, from floor to ceiling - **gold**, and this gold glowed with powerful energy, and it hummed with electricity. For nobody knew, but Lou's home was the only source known of this rare voltaic mineral - able to catch the sun's light and hold on to its power.

"How much do I take?" Pico asked.

"Take all that you need!" guffawed the happy lizard.

Well, not even all the dust off the floor could Pico's pouch hold, but she took what she could, scooping it up with her two cupped hands. Then satisfied, she slung her pouch over her shoulder, and Lou stooped low so she could climb up on her back. Pico held her arms around the dragon's neck, as the great lizard carried her out the cave's entrance, down the beach, and entered the water, easily as a crocodile slips from the shore. Old Lou was a masterful swimmer, and Pico clung tightly, as she glided powerfully out to the deep with a few quick flicks of her tail. Pico rolled her head around and gazed up at the stars. What a night! It was as if the sky and the sea had become one, and she was riding out across the Milky Way.

"You know what," Pico confided to Lou. "You're not that scary."

"Oh, I'm a little loony," chuckled Lou, "but I'm not scary."

Pico was having the time of her life. Just imagine what her friends would say. Who would believe her - her, Pico, on the back of a dragon, with a bag full of gold! "Sure you did," they'd say. Yes, she was almost in heaven, millions of miles away, riding across the sky from star to star. It was only the sound of Lou's deep voice beneath her that brought her back down to earth.

"Well, Pico," she said. "The sun's about to come up, and I need to be back in my cave."

"But I'm having so much fun!" hollered Pico. "I don't want this to end."

"Well, nothing lasts forever," Lou told her, "just enjoy it while you can kid. Just enjoy it while you can." Then with one easy stride, the dragon came up onshore, leaned over, and let Pico slide off her back, and without waiting for thanks, or even goodbye, she plunged back into the water from where she came, and swam off into the darkness towards her cave. Her laughter echoed across the water as she went.

Dawn approached, and the moon slipped back down into the sea. Pico was only a short distance from her plane. As she crossed the dunes, the sun's first rays were just filling the sky, and David was standing there, awaiting her return. Her plane remained stuck, ploughed into the sand as she'd left it.

Pico could hardly contain her excitement. "Wow David!" she said. "You really were right. Those really were the best three days of my life. We did so many fun things. We climbed trees. We saw that great parrot. We went on a canoe ride. I got the treasure. I even rode on the back of a dragon!"

The kindly old man smiled. "Yes, I told you, after those three days you wouldn't want to leave."

Pico was torn. "Yes, it is true," she said, "but I guess it is time for me to leave."

"You know - you could always stay," suggested David. "I have rather enjoyed your company - someone to have a yarn with."

"The idea did cross my mind," admitted Pico, "but I do like my life - the places I go, the people I meet, the adventures I have, and besides, I still have parcels to deliver." Then she had a thought. "Hey, why don't you come with me?"

The old man shook his head. He too had thought of it. "But I've lived on this island so long," he said, "I don't think I could go back to that other way of living, and besides, if I leave, who is going to document all the new species of plants and birds. No Pico, I'll stay, but do come and visit me won't you?"

Pico felt a little lump in her throat. She had become rather fond of the old man in those three days. "Oh I'll come and visit you for sure," she promised. "But David, how will I find you?"

David got a far away look in his eyes and said, "you'll find me Pico, when you're not looking for me. Happy trails kid, happy trails."

And with that, the old islander turned, and strolled his way up to the top of the beach. There he waved, and stood watching, as Pico took up her treasure and walked over to her plane.

"Well, I guess I just take some of this treasure, sprinkle it on my plane, and then my plane will be powered by the sun. Do you hear that Sun!" Pico called out. "You are going to power my plane!" She still couldn't quite believe it but, "oh well, I guess it's worth a try," she said.

Taking the fine gold in her hand, she proceeded to give her plane a thorough dusting. She spread it over the wings to give it lift. She spread it over the tail for stability, and she spread it over the engine and propeller to give it thrust. As she sprinkled the gold it glittered in the morning sun, before falling onto the plane's yellow skin, adding a splendid glow to its finish.

Finally, Pico climbed into the cockpit and sprinkled the last of the treasure over the controls. "Well, here goes," she said, and began flicking on the switches. Her dash lights came on, and it was all systems go. Now it was the moment of truth. "Contact," she said, and hit the ignition.

But nothing happened - no roaring into action of the motor, just quiet. Pico's heart sank. Then slowly, she looked up, and to her surprise, the propeller was moving. It was working! Only, the electric motor was so quiet, she couldn't hear it running - just a low hum, that was all.

Pico got excited and pulled the throttle. The propeller sped up. Now she could hear the wind beating in its blades. She gave it a little bit more, and slowly the plane pulled itself from the deep sands, and began to roll along the beach. This was it. Pico opened up the throttle and the plane lurched, running faster and faster, full tilt towards the mouth of the lagoon. And at the very last moment, Pico pulled back on the controls, and the plane lifted off, soaring high out over the blue waters.

Pico would never have believed it. Her plane was running on the energy of the sun - so clean, and so quiet! She would never run out of fuel again, and it was all thanks to the generosity of the sun, with a little help from David, and Lou's special treasure of course.

As she gained altitude, Pico pulled hard over to the side to do one last circle of the island. She looked down, and could see David still standing there, waving up to her from the beach. Crossing over the lagoon, she could see the mouth of Lou's cave, and beyond to the forest where they had climbed trees and spotted that parrot. It had been a magical three days she would never forget!

Then, high above the island, she took the controls once more and levelled off. She checked her compass and found her bearing, before stealing one last glance behind, to see if it had not all been a dream. Then she took the microphone, and called out over the radio. ***"Pico to home base**, **this is Pico to home base***. I'm airborne again. I repeat. Airborne again, and I'm flying off, into the distance."

The End

CPSIA information can be obtained
at www.ICGtesting.com
Printed in the USA
BVHW091326180522
637192BV00003B/50